I0521192

The Innkeeper's Wife

A Dramatic Monolog for Advent
or Christmas Eve
By Harriet Faust

C.S.S. Publishing Co., Inc.

Lima, Ohio

THE INNKEEPER'S WIFE: A SOLILOQUY

Reprinted 2002

Copyright © 1990 by
CSS Publishing Company, Inc.
Lima, Ohio

For more information about CSS Publishing Company resources, visit our website at www.csspub.com or e-mail us at custserv@csspub.com or call (800) 241-4056.

ISBN 1-55673-255-4   PRINTED IN U.S.A.

— Suggestions for Staging —

There are many creative possibilities for staging this monolog, some elaborate, some quite simple. One possibility is to arrange for one person to read Miriam's soliloquy offstage, while actors costumed in period clothing portray the action silently onstage. This could be particularly effective if done on a darkened set with a single spotlight, simulating Miriam's recollections.

Another possibility is to prepare slides or videotape of the story's action in advance. You can also tape the monolog, if care is given to synchronize sound and image. This approach relieves your cast of onstage pressure while providing a meaningful experience for your audience.

Finally, if you are short on both volunteers and resources, you may wish to use the monolog alone, without actors, sets, or costumes. Your reader should be onstage in this case, and may read from a script or cue cards.

These suggestions are certainly not exhaustive, and you are likely to find that your group can brainstorm a number of innovative improvements and original approaches in a very short time.

— The Innkeeper's Wife —

My name is Miriam.
I am the innkeeper's wife.
This inn has always been my home.
In fact, I was born in that little room
Back there under the eaves.

I grew up in this inn.
It belonged to my father, Ephraim,
Who married my mother, Keturah.

I love this inn,
Every dusty corner of it.
It was here I played as a child.
It was here I listened to the tales
Of those who traveled through our city.

For Bethlehem is a stopping place
For caravans traveling
From Nazareth to Jerusalem
And lands farther away.

I loved those caravans,
Their camels loaded with
Dates and figs,
And rugs of bright and lustrous colors,

And olive oil, and delicious-smelling perfumes.
But, most of all, I loved the stories
The travelers told to all who would listen.
And I listened.

Listened as they pictured for me
The Holy City of Jerusalem,
Where some day I would go with my parents
To keep the Passover Feast.
How I longed to see the Temple
With its beautiful furnishings.
The Temple built to honor Jehovah,
The God of Abraham, Isaac, and Jacob.

And our God, too.
For we were devout Hebrews
Who carefully
And joyfully
Celebrated all the Holy Days as they came.

Sometimes there came a traveler
From lands far, far away
Who loved to tell of the glory that was past
In those lands of the East.
They told of ancient Babylon,
With its thick walls
On which soldiers had stood
To guard their city.

Babylon — with its beautiful river
Bright as silver,
Running underneath the walls.
Babylon with its temples,
Its fruit trees,
Its handsome chariots.

Sometimes travelers came
From far-off Egypt.
Men who had seen the ancient pyramids,
Men who had been at the spot
Where Moses parted the waters,

So my ancestors could escape
On dry land.
While the Egyptians following them
Were drowned in the sea.

With the story-tellers I could see
Old Mt. Sinai
And Moses coming down from the mount
With his white beard and his flowing robes,
Moses with those precious tablets of stone
Whereon were written
The Ten Commandments.

I loved those stories
But most of all, I loved to hear
About the Promise —

The Promise — that some day
The Messiah would come
To my people.

The Messiah — would he come
In robes of glory,
With precious jewels crowning his head?
Would he come with camel caravans
Bearing precious burdens?
Would there be soldiers with spears?
Would there be trumpets sounding?
Would all of us fall down
And worship him?

My father, Ephraim, had waited for the Messiah,
But my father died,
Then my mother, Keturah.
Still the Messiah had not come.

I was grown up then
And the inn was mine.
Mine and Simon's,
The lad of whom my parents approved,
The lad to whom I had given my hand in marriage.

Travelers still came to the inn,
Day after day,
Month after month.

And always I listened to them
Telling of the Promise
Of the Messiah.

Would he stop at this inn, I wondered.
How I hoped he would.
I could almost see him come
In all his glory.

So, one day I made a room ready for him
With our best and whitest linens,
And a soft pillow for his head,
And handsome bowls
Upon the table.

But the Messiah did not come.
And, one day, tired and weary of waiting,
I made a decision.
By this time Simon and I
Had become the parents of Lydia,
Our precious daughter.

Lydia, with her gentle, loving ways
And her sparkling laughter.
How we loved her, our only child.
She would sleep beneath those coverlets.
And the bowls of brass and silver
On the table would be hers to enjoy.

Lydia loved that room.
But, most of all, she loved to roam in the garden,
And along the paths through the fields
Laden with grain.

She loved to listen to the turtledoves
Singing in the branches of the olive trees.
She loved to listen to the rippling waters
In wayside streams.

Lydia, our daughter, was an outdoor girl
With the fragrance of flowers and grasses
Floating out from the robes she wore.

There came a day when Lydia appeared before us
Clasping the hand of Nathan, a shepherd lad.
Lydia, with her sparkling eyes;
And Nathan, quiet and gentle,
Had come to ask for Lydia's hand in marriage.
How shocked we were!
How disappointed!
We had counted on her marriage to Andrew,
Who worked in metals.

Andrew's father and Lydia's father
Had had an understanding for years.
How could these thoughtless young people
Disregard all that their parents had planned for them?

I was angry, Simon was sad.
But, in the end, he gave his consent,
For it was beyond him to deny
His beautiful daughter anything.

In the midst of my anger
They went away
To live in a shepherd's cottage
Among the hills
Outside of Bethlehem.

Two years passed by,
Two lonely, lonely years.
"Other mothers have their daughters with them on feast days,"
I complained to Simon.
"Why doesn't she come?"

"Lydia will not come where Nathan isn't welcome,"
Simon explained with pain in his eyes.
Simon had grown silent since Lydia went away —
And we did not talk and laugh together
As we had in days gone by.

I know he missed our daughter sorely,
But I missed her more.
For I was Lydia's mother,
The mother of a daughter she never, never saw.

Then, one day, something different came to pass;
In a caravan from far away there came a boy,
Tired and pale, dragging one foot after the other.
"It's hard for him to travel with us,"
Explained the caravan's leader.
"We brought him only because
He had no place else to go."

Simon looked upon the homeless lad,
And his great heart swelled with pity.
"Leave him here," he begged.
"He can help me at the inn,
He can tend the camels
And help keep the inn in order.
I'll take care of him
Until he is grown."
And so our inn
Became a home for Reuben.

I must confess
I did not like the lad.
He was thin and pale,
And he dragged one foot after the other.
And he seldom, or never, smiled.

Simon, sensing my dislike, kept the boy
Out of my sight as much as possible.
Simon saw that he was fed,
And the boy slept in a little stable-cave,
Warm and comfortable.

Sometimes I heard Simon and Reuben
Laughing and talking together.
But I did not ask why they were merry.

My days were too full of missing Lydia.
Every day I missed her more.
I kept her room locked against all intruders.
It became a precious shrine to me.

But, sometimes, when there was no one to see me,
I unlocked that door and went in
All by myself.
I touched the linen sheets
And the soft pillow.
I dusted the precious bowls upon the table.
But mostly I wept,
Wept for the daughter I had lost.

One night, as I locked the door,
After an hour of weeping,
Reuben approached me,
Walking across the courtyard,
Dragging one foot after the other.
I shuddered with dislike.
Why was he coming to me,
That uncouth lad?

Reuben was speaking in a soft, halting voice,
"My master sent me to tell you a young man
And a maiden have come from afar
Seeking shelter at the inn.
They are in need, for a baby is to be born
And the inn is full.
He asks, 'Will you open Lydia's room for them
Just for tonight?' "

Sudden anger surged through my being —
Lydia's beautiful room given to strangers!
What could Simon be thinking of?
He knew how I felt about Lydia's room.
How could he ask such an outrageous question?

"Go tell your master," I said to Reuben,
"I will not have strangers in Lydia's room."

Reuben turned away, then turned back
As if he would plead their cause.
But I cried out,
"There is nothing more to be said,
Go, give your master my answer."

Still shaken with anger,
I watched as Reuben shuffled off
Across the courtyard,
Painfully carrying my answer to his master.

For just a minute I considered
Calling the lad back
And bidding him tell Simon
The room could house the strangers,
Just for one night.

But, no, I could not do that.
My pain over Lydia
Was far too deep.
That's all I had left of my daughter,
That little room under the eaves.

After a while I lay down on my pallet
Near the door
And tried to sleep.

Simon would be late, for the town was full of people,
People coming to register in the town of their birth.
Because of a new law they had come,
The law of Caesar Augustus.

After a while the noise died down
And I fell into uneasy slumber.

Then, suddenly, I was awakened,
Awakened by voices just outside my door.
Simon was speaking, and the other?
It was Nathan, Lydia's husband.
What could he be doing here?

I sat bolt upright,
My hands at my temples.
Could something have happened to my precious daughter?

Nathan's voice was gentle, soothing,
The voice I remembered.
But there was something different tonight,
That soft voice was filled with excitement,
With overwhelming wonder!

"I wish you could have been there,"
Nathan was speaking to Simon.
"We were out on the hillside
Keeping watch over our flocks this night.

When right before our eyes,
An angel appeared unto us,
And a brilliant light shone all around us,
And we were sore afraid.

But the angel said unto us,
'Fear not for I bring you tidings of great joy
Which shall be to all people.

'For unto you is born this day,
In the City of David,
A Savior who is Christ, the Lord.
And this shall be a sign unto you:

'You shall find the Babe
Wrapped in swaddling clothes
And lying in a manger.'

"And, suddenly, Simon, there was with the angel
A multitude of the heavenly host
Praising God and saying,
'Glory to God in the highest,
And, on earth, peace, goodwill to men.'

"And, when the angels went back into heaven,
The bright light died,
And we said one to another,
'Let us go to Bethlehem
And see this thing that has come to pass.'

"So we came with haste,
And, in the manger, your manger, Simon,
We found the Babe wrapped in swaddling clothes."

The voices died away,
But I sat there, shaking my head in disbelief.

A Babe, heralded by angels!
It must be, it had to be the Messiah!
The Messiah for whom I had been waiting
Nearly all the years of my life.

The Messiah had come to the stable!
Simon's stable!
It was not to me the angels had spoken,
But to Nathan and the other shepherds!

I was shaken with disappointment and anger.
Angels had come to Nathan whom I disliked,
Nathan, who had taken my daughter away from me!

Why had they not come to me?
It was I who had listened to travelers
Telling of the promise of the Messiah!
It was I who had once prepared a room for him,
Hoping he would sleep on my white sheets,
And rest his head upon my soft pillow!

It was not Simon, or Nathan, or Reuben —
It was I who had been waiting for the *promise!*

I slept no more that night.
But it was almost noon
When I knew I must go to the stable.
I had to see for myself
That which had come to pass.

As I entered the dim stable,
All was quiet and still.
The fragrance of clean, dry grasses
Surrounded the place.
The breath of slow-breathing animals
Was in the air.
Doves cooed softly
From their perches above the manger.

In the quiet place I wondered
If the family had gone away, or
Maybe this was just a dream I had dreamed.

Then, suddenly, I heard a cry from the manger,
A baby's cry!
No mother can mistake a baby's cry
For anything else!

The story was true
Just as Nathan had told it.

Fearfully, I crept closer.
Then, in the stillness,
A soft voice began to sing.

The singing stopped
And all was quiet.
Fearfully, I crept closer.

"Don't be afraid,"
A soft voice soothed away my fears.
And I saw the mother,
Her face shining with a strange beauty.
Her voice held all the music
Of birds singing in the springtime.

I stopped, for I knew I was unworthy,
Unworthy of looking upon the face
Of the Babe in the manger.
I, whose heart was filled with hatred
Toward Simon, toward Lydia, toward Nathan,
And Reuben who lived in the inn.

"Reuben," the soft voice spoke
The name of the crippled lad.
As if she knew what I was thinking,
The voice went on,
"Reuben, the lad who found this stable for us,
And brought clean hay
To make a bed for the child.
Come, you must see the Babe,
Reach out your hands and caress him."

But, again, I shrank away.
Then, suddenly, I knew
This could be a new beginning
For me, Miriam,
Who had been the cause of so much unhappiness.

"I will try to make up for it all,"
I whispered brokenly.
"I will be kind to Simon, and to Nathan,
And to Lydia,
And to Reuben, the crippled lad."

I paused, and the beautiful voice spoke again,
As if she knew what I was thinking.

"Lydia's room can be Reuben's room,"
She told me,
"And you will come to love the lad
Just as Simon loves him."

"But I did nothing for the Baby," I cried,
My heart torn with dark remorse.

"There will be other babies,"
The gentle mother told me.
"All your life there will be others
Who need your help.
In helping them, you will be helping
Your Father, God, who sent the Babe to earth."

"In helping them I will be helping him,"
I said the words aloud.
And, suddenly, the heavy burden lifted,
I was free from the weight of the past.

I knelt before the manger,
Knowing the truth in my inmost heart:
Helping others will be helping him,
The Babe in the manger,
And the Father above.

Never again would I be bitter
And unloving.
The years spread out before my eyes,
Years in which I could bring rest for the weary
In this very inn.
Years in which I may feed the hungry
And clothe the poor.

With one last look
At the Babe and his mother,
I left the stable,
Eager now to begin
A new and different life.

Outside the stable the sun shone
Brightly.
And, deep inside me, was a brightness
All its own.
The Promise had come to me
After all.

www.ingramcontent.com/pod-product-compliance
Lightning Source LLC
Chambersburg PA
CBHW071232130626
46555CB00004B/1953